Guthli has Wings

Guthli has Wings

Kanak Shashi

Guthli lived with her Ma, Papa, brother and sister. She was the youngest in the family.

Guthli was a chatterbox. She would draw fairies, and roam the Satpura hills for hours, collecting leaves of different kinds. She was happiest swinging on swings and climbing trees. Guthli had her cycle that she rode everywhere. She knew how to oil it and fill air in the tyre, and keep it in top shape.

At home she was everyone's favourite. And when her mother called her sonchiriya, her golden bird, she would turn as red as a pomegranate.

It was Diwali the next day, and everyone was busy decorating the house. Guthli was making a rangoli with her sister. There were new clothes for everyone.

But Guthli was not happy with her clothes. She liked the light, frilly frock that her sister had been given. Quietly she wore it and then went out to show everyone.

"Why are you wearing my new frock?" her sister screamed. Her brother burst out laughing and Papa looked at her with angry eyes. Guthli's eyes filled up.

Ma took her inside and hugged her.

Then gently she said, "Son, you are a boy. You should wear your own clothes, not your sister's."

"But I want to be a fairy! And why do you keep saying I'm a boy when I'm a girl?"

"Because you are like your brother, not like your sister. Boys are boys and girls are girls, Guthli."

"No-no, I'm a fairy!" Guthli was adamant.

"Boys are not fairies, they are princes. And you are the most handsome, sweet little prince in the whole world." Ma gave him a hug.

Guthli separated herself from her mother's hug. "I'm not a prince. I'm a girl and I'm a fairy and I want to wear this dress."

Ma's voice was angry now. "Don't be stubborn. You are a boy. Now go and change out of your frock," she said and went out.

All through Diwali, Guthli was sad. Even amidst the noise of crackers, the glowing diyas, and the food and sweets, she felt alone. Lost in her own thoughts, away from everyone else's laughter and happiness.

After this, Guthli grew very quiet and began to stay by herself.

She would talk only to the trees and leaves among which she roamed. And to a few little chickens that she was friends with.

The sound of her chatter vanished from the house.

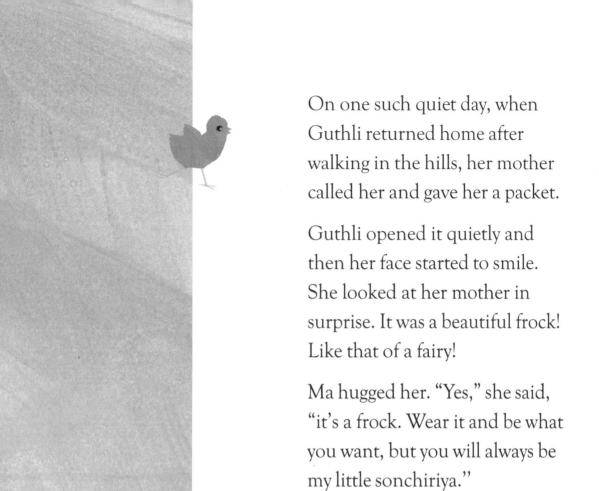

On one such quiet day, when Guthli returned home after walking in the hills, her mother called her and gave her a packet.

Guthli opened it quietly and then her face started to smile. She looked at her mother in surprise. It was a beautiful frock! Like that of a fairy!

Ma hugged her. "Yes," she said, "it's a frock. Wear it and be what you want, but you will always be my little sonchiriya."

Guthli held the frock tight and buried her
head in her mother's hug.

Then she wore her frock and danced.
She was happy. She was a golden bird
and could fly high up in the sky, over all
the rules of the world. Rules that said she
was a boy because she was born with a boy's
body, and not the girl she *knew* she was.

She felt like a real fairy now.

Slowly she would change the world.
For today, this was enough.

Guthli Has Wings

ISBN 978-93-86667-94-6
© Kanak Shashi
First published in India, 2019

The story previously appeared in the anthology Being Boys *by Tulika. It has also been published as a picture book in a set of graded readers by Muskaan, an organisation working with marginalised children and their communities in Bhopal.*

Published by
Tulika Publishers, 305 Manickam Avenue, TTK Road, Alwarpet, Chennai 600 018, India
email reachus@tulikabooks.com *website* www.tulikabooks.com

Printed and bound by
Sterling and Quadra Press India Ltd, Chennai 600 024, India